Second U.S. edition 1998

Based on the book *Guess How Much I Love You*™ by Sam McBratney,
first published in the U.S. by Candlewick Press, 1995.

ISBN 978-0-7636-1909-1

12 14 16 18 20 19 17 15 13

Printed in Italy

Candlewick Press
2067 Massachusetts Avenue
Cambridge, Massachusetts 02140

visit us at www.candlewick.com

MY BABY BOOK

illustrated by
Anita Jeram

—— *Based on* ——

GUESS HOW MUCH I LOVE YOU™

written by
Sam McBratney

MY FAMILY

*Before there was me,
there was the rest of my family . . .*

My mom: _____ .

Her birth date: _____ .

My dad: _____ .

His birth date: _____ .

The names and birth dates of some other

people in my family:

_____

_____

_____

_____ .

Here are some pictures of my family.

Place pictures here

Guess how much I love them all!
And guess how much
they love me!

MY FIRST NINE MONTHS

Mom and Dad first found out they were expecting me in the month of _____ .

The name of Mom's doctor

was _____ .

Mom thought I would be a

girl ☐   boy ☐

Dad thought I would be a

girl ☐   boy ☐

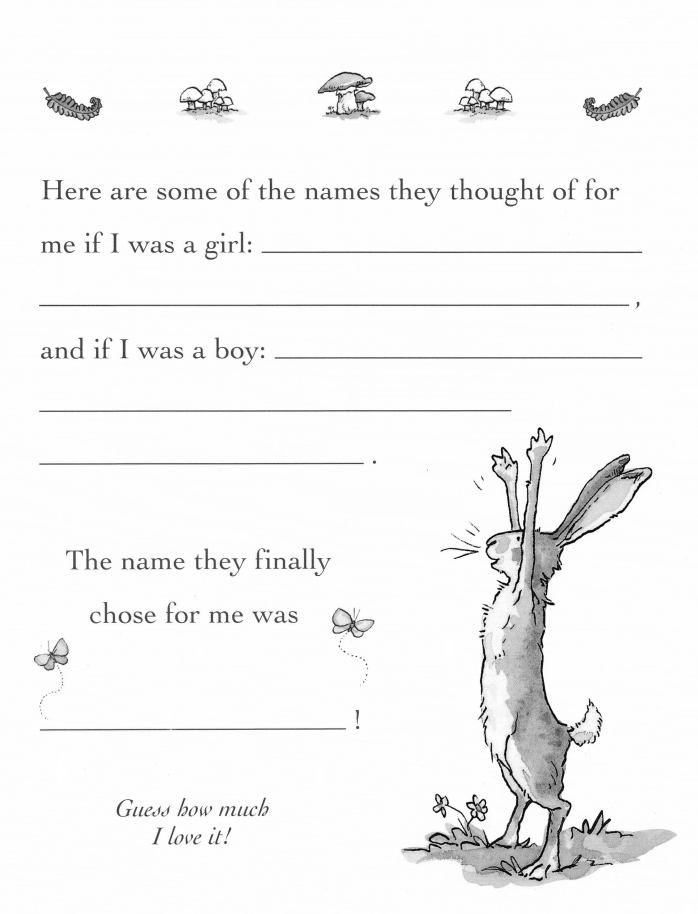

Here are some of the names they thought of for me if I was a girl: _____ _____,
and if I was a boy: _____
_____
_____ .

The name they finally chose for me was

_____ !

*Guess how much
I love it!*

Here is a picture of Mom when she was expecting me.

Place picture here

While she was expecting me, Mom *loved*

these foods: _____

_____ .

And she *hated* these foods: _____

_____ .

Some ways Mom and Dad got ready for

my arrival were _____

_____

_____ .

The date they first heard my heartbeat

was _____ .

The date they first felt me kick

was _____ .

The date I was due to be born

was _____ .

Guess how excited we all were as
that date came closer.
Soon we would all meet!

BEING BORN

At last! I was born!

The date I arrived was

_____ .

So now that's my birthday!

The place was

_____

_____

_____

_____ .

When I was born it was

night  day

The time was

_____ .

ME

Here is the first picture of me ever!

Place picture here

Guess what I was like when I was born!

I weighed _____ . I measured _____ .

The color of my eyes was _____ .

The color of my hair was _____ .

Mom said I looked like _____ .

Dad said I looked like _____ .

Other people said I looked like _____

_____

_____ .

*Guess who I think
I looked like?
ME!*

15

FIRST DAYS

Mom and Dad told everybody about me!

Some first gifts I was given were

_____

_____

_____ .

The first car I

ever rode in was a

_____ .

*Guess how sleepy
I was when I was new!*

My first home was at

_____

_____

_____ .

16

Here are the autographs of some of the first people I ever met: _____

_____

_____

The first song that was ever sung to me was _____ .

Guess how much I loved it!

KEEPSAKES

My newspaper announcement

My name bracelet

My birth announcement

MY FIRST FOOTPRINTS

Here are my baby footprints! Aren't they tiny?

Guess how much everyone loved me.

All the way up to my toes!

OTHER NEWS

*Guess what other things were going on
in the world when I was born.*

Our leader was _____ .

Other leaders around the world were _____

_____ .

The clothes in style were _____

_____ .

Some hit songs were _____

_____ .

Some famous movie stars were _____

_____ .

Some famous athletes were

_____

_____

_____ .

20

Here is a picture of me, after my
first week in the world!

Place picture here

A newspaper cost _____ , a movie ticket

cost _____ , and a gallon of milk cost _____ .

A postage stamp

looked like this:

FIRST BABY FEATS

I first slept through the night when

I was _____ old.

I first smiled when

I was _____ old.

I first discovered my hands when

I was _____ old.

I first grasped something when

I was _____ old.

I first discovered my feet when

I was _____ old.

I first clapped when

I was _____ old.

I first waved bye-bye when

I was _____ old.

Guess how much I loved being tickled!

 EATING

The first solid food I ever tasted

was _____ .

My first tooth came in on _____ .

My second tooth came in on _____ .

My third tooth came in on _____ .

My fourth tooth came in on _____ .

I first drank from a cup when

I was _____ old.

I first used a spoon when

I was _____ old.

My favorite things to eat were

_____

_____

_____ .

Yum!

My least favorite things to eat

were _____

_____

_____ .

Yuck!

UP AND ABOUT

I first held my head up when

I was _____ old.

I first rolled over when

I was _____ old.

I first sat up alone when

I was _____ old.

I first crawled when

I was _____ old.

I could pull up to standing when

I was _____ old.

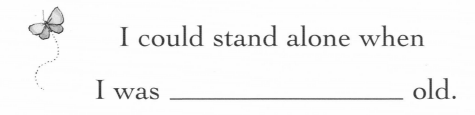

I could stand alone when

I was _____ old.

At last! I took my first step when

I was _____ old.

Guess how often I fell over! Oops-a-daisy!

TALKING

 My first word *ever* was

_____ .

My first name for Mom was _____ ,

and my first name for Dad was _____ .

Some of my other first words

were _____

_____ .

My favorite rhymes to say

were _____

_____ .

My favorite songs to sing

were _____

_____

_____ .

Guess how much I loved talking!

29

 # PLAYING

My first friends were _____

_____ .

My favorite toys were _____

_____ .

My favorite things to

do outside were

_____

_____

_____

_____ .

My favorite bedtime books were _____

_____ .

CELEBRATING

The holidays our family celebrated were

_____ .

The first holiday we celebrated after I was born

was _____ .

Gifts I received that day were _____

_____

_____ .

Some happy things
that happened were

_____

_____

_____

_____ .

BUMPS AND BRUISES

 Sometimes I got sick or hurt myself.

Some first illnesses I had

were _____

_____

_____ .

My doctor's name was

_____ .

Some baby medicines I had to take

 were _____

_____ .

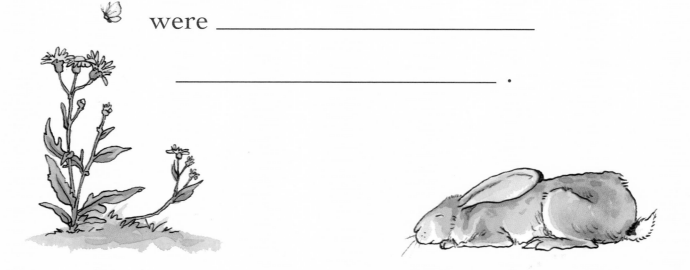

Some illnesses I was immunized against

were _____

_____

_____ .

Some bumps and falls I had

were _____

_____

_____ .

Guess how much I liked
being kissed better!

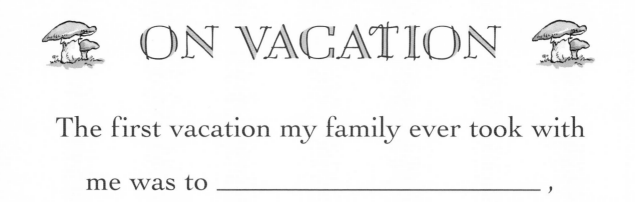

ON VACATION

The first vacation my family ever took with

me was to _____ ,

when I was _____ old.

Some adventures we had

were _____

_____

_____

_____ .

Here are some pictures of us on vacation.

Place pictures here

Guess how much I love vacations!
Across the river and over the hills!

❧ MY FIRST BIRTHDAY ❧

*Happy hoppy
birthday!*

People who sang "Happy Birthday"

to me that day were _____

_____ .

Special birthday things we ate

were _____ .

Some gifts I was given were _____

_____

_____ .

Place picture here

Here I am exactly one year old!

MY SECOND BIRTHDAY

Here I am exactly two years old!

Place picture here

Some gifts I was given that day were

_____ .

Games we played were _____

_____

_____ .

Songs we sang

were _____

_____

_____

_____ .

*How big I was
starting to grow . . .*

GROWING

I grew and grew — I couldn't stop!

Date	Age	Height	Weight
_____	_____	_____	_____
_____	_____	_____	_____
_____	_____	_____	_____
_____	_____	_____	_____
_____	_____	_____	_____
_____	_____	_____	_____
_____	_____	_____	_____
_____	_____	_____	_____

I could never have done it without my family!
They helped me all the way . . .

Guess how much I love them —
right up to the moon!

And guess how much
they love me — right up to the
moon and back!

SPECIAL MEMORIES

Here are some special pictures and memories . . .

of other things we did when I was small . . .

Guess how much
I'll treasure
them . . .

one day when
I've grown
tall!

45